this ORQ. (he cave boy.)

David Elliott

illustrated by Lori Nichols

BOYDS MILLS PRESS
AN IMPRINT OF HIGHLIGHTS
Honesdale, Pennsylvania

This for Don and Joyce.
They in-laws. They terrific.
—DE

For Ken
(Kenny BIG hero. Lori love Kenny.)
—LN

Text copyright © 2014 by David Elliott
Illustrations copyright © 2014 by Lori Nichols
For information about permission to reproduce selections
from this book, contact permissions@highlights.com.

Boyds Mills Press
An Imprint of Highlights
815 Church Street
Honesdale, Pennsylvania 18431

Printed in China
ISBN: 978-1-62091-521-9
Library of Congress Control Number: 2014931588

First edition

Designed by Anahid Hamparian
Production by Margaret Mosomillo
The text of this book is set in Neutraface.
The illustrations are done in #4 pencil on Strathmore drawing paper and colorized digitally.
10 9 8 7 6 5 4 3 2 1

Special thanks to the illustrator's young friends HZ&B, PK, and Suzanna
for being willing to strike a pose at the drop of a hat. And thanks to KM
for the prehistoric bird banter. —LN

This Orq.

He live in cave.

He carry club.

He cave boy.

This Woma.

Woma woolly mammoth.

Orq **love** Woma.

Every day Woma grow **bigger** ...

and **bigger** …

... and
bigger!

Orq
love
Woma.

But Orq's mother
not convinced.
Woma shed.

Woma smell.

Woma not house-trained.

Mother say,
"Get that woolly
mammoth out of
this cave!"

Poor Woma.

Orq **love** Woma.

Orq get **big** idea.
Teach Woma tricks.

Mother think Woma smart.

Mother think Woma cute.

Mother *love* Woma.

"Speak, Woma! Speak!"

"Fetch, Woma! Fetch!"

"Roll over, Woma! Roll o—"

Poor Woma!

Orq **love** Woma.

One day, Orq playing.

He mighty hunter!

Hunt bison!

Hunt cave bear!

Hunt . . .

. . . sabertooth!

Poor Orq!

Sabertooth **love** Orq. But . . .

. . . Woma **love** Orq more!
Sabertooth reconsider.

Orq safe now.

Woma **big** hero.

Mother **love** Woma.
Woma back in cave.

Kind of.